Triple Trouble
for Rupert

By ETHELYN M. PARKINSON

Illustrated by Mary Stevens

SCHOLASTIC BOOK SERVICES

Published by Scholastic Book Services, a division
of Scholastic Magazines, Inc., New York, N.Y.

The characters in this book first appeared in stories published in "Trailblazer."

Single copy price 35¢. Quantity prices available on request.

Copyright 1953, 1956, 1957, 1958, 1959, 1960, by W. L. Jenkins. Copyright © 1960, by Scholastic Magazines, Inc. Published by Scholastic Book Services.

4th printing................February 1963

Printed in the U.S.A.

CONTENTS

For My Nephew

Bruce

A Tale of the Sea

MAYBE this is a man's world, but at Lincoln School there is only a small corner that belongs to the guys, and that is the "No Dames" corner.

People like Opal Duncan and Smart Annabelle Willman and Beautiful Sylvia Singer can stand around and listen, but they cannot come in.

"We have to do something about spies," Milt Morrissey said. "They are against the law."

But just then the bell rang.

When we went in, Miss Carlman was wearing her company smile and Miss Mildred Amory was sitting in the extra chair. Miss Amory is a school supervisor, and we could see that Miss Carlman wanted us to make a keen impression on her.

Clayton Snow poked me. "On guard, Piper!" he said.

Miss Carlman shook her head at us. That meant, "Clayton Snow and Rupert Piper, quiet!" She did not want to say it before company.

Miss Carlman is very proud of the sixth grade, and when we have company we have to show off.

"We have been studying transportation and communication," she said. "We will have a little review. What does transportation mean?"

Sylvia waved. "Transportation is carrying people or objects from place to place."

"And can you name some early means of transportation?"

"Covered wagons," Sylvia said. "And stagecoaches."

"Excellent!" said Miss Carlman. "Opal, please name another."

Opal thought and thought. "Station wagons?" she said, through her nose.

Opal has a very one-track mind, and her dad has just bought a station wagon.

Trowbridge "Doodleberries" Hall was waving.

"Yes, Trowbridge?" Miss Carlman said.

Dood stood up. "DC-7's, and Flying Boxcars," he said.

"Oh, my!" said Miss Amory. "Did you really study those?"

"A little," Miss Carlman laughed. "Annabelle, can you name some other kinds of transportation?"

Smart Annabelle stood up. "Canoes and small boats," she said. "Barges and steamboats on the rivers. Ocean liners. Railroads, freight and passenger trains. Dray lines and trucks. Passenger buses."

"Excellent!" Miss Carlman smiled. "And now, Rupert, what is communication?"

I recited. "Communication is passing and exchanging messages."

"Very good," said Miss Carlman. "Who will name an early means of communication?"

Clayte waved. "Writing, and the pony express."

"Very good," said Miss Carlman. "Who can name some later ones?"

Milt waved. "Telephone, telegraph, tell-a-woman!" he said.

Everybody laughed because this was a joke, and Miss Amory laughed hardest of all.

Miss Carlman looked proud. Then she said, "There are a few important means of communication that we have not mentioned."

I waved, but of course Smart Annabelle waved harder.

"Yes, Annabelle?"

"Radio and TV," said Annabelle. She flipped her eyelashes at me. "Also, light signals, flag signals and smoke signals."

"Very good!" said Miss Carlman. "Rupert?"

Well, I was mad. Annabelle had said everything I was going to say. But I did not want to tell Miss Carlman that, because Annabelle feels smart enough anyway.

I thought very fast. "A message in a bottle," I said.

Everybody stared at me. Annabelle stared hardest.

My eyelashes are not as long as hers, but I flipped them at her.

Then I gave Miss Carlman a very sweet smile. She did not smile back.

She only said, "We will have a review of fractions."

But Miss Amory looked at her watch and stood up.

"Miss Carlman," she said, "my time is up. I have certainly enjoyed being here, boys and girls. You have a very fine class and are doing some very nice work. Good-by."

So we all stood up, the way Miss Carlman taught us, until Miss Amory left the room.

Then Miss Carlman looked at me. She looked at me all through arithmetic.

"Ready for recess," she said. "Rupert Piper, you will remain in your seat."

Milt and Dood and Clayte are very true friends. They stayed outside the door, to help me suffer. Opal stayed, too, but she only wanted to listen.

"Rupert," Miss Carlman said, "come up here. We are going to have a little talk."

I smiled at her. "That is a very good means of communication," I said.

"I do not feel very funny," she told me. "Rupert, I am not proud of your last recitation. I just wonder if Miss Amory thinks that I taught you that a message in a bottle is an important means of communication."

"I am sure you would have told me," I said. "But maybe you did not know. My Uncle Hugo told me."

"Indeed!" said Miss Carlman. "Do tell me more."

"Well, my Uncle Hugo got shipwrecked," I said. "His boat struck a rock and was broken all to pieces."

"Indeed!" she said.

"So," I said, "Uncle Hugo swam and swam until he was washed ashore on an island." I closed my eyes, because Miss Carlman was looking at me so hard I could not see the island.

"Go on," she said. "I am spellbound. It was a very beautiful island, I suppose, with palm trees and strange crimson flowers, and with screaming birds and monkeys, but no sign of human life."

I opened my eyes a little and peeked at her. "No, Miss Carlman," I said, "that is not quite right. It was just an old rocky island. All rocks. And there were some sea gulls, but no monkeys."

I shut my eyes again. "And there sat Uncle Hugo, all alone on this cold island, with no shelter and with a cold wind blowing. Winter was coming, and Uncle Hugo was afraid he would perish and become a lifeless form."

"Rupert," Miss Carlman said, "I know I am asking a great deal, but open your eyes and look at me — and then see if you care to go on with this tale of the sea."

I peeked at her. Miss Carlman does not look like my Mom, but sometimes she looks as if she is thinking the same things.

"But I didn't finish," I said.

"Boys!" Miss Carlman called, "you are supposed to be out playing ball. But as long as you have stayed right on the job, you may come in and take your seats. You too, Opal. And Annabelle, and Sylvia, and the rest. It would be a shame to waste Rupert's story on one teacher."

"Miss Carlman," I said, "the guys — I mean the boys

— know this story. The girls know it too, I guess, because Opal was standing around the 'No Dames' corner, listening."

"Well," Miss Carlman said, "it probably gets better every time it is told. You may continue. I can see some little problems coming up, and I wonder how you and Uncle Hugo are going to solve them."

"Where was I?" I said.

"Winter was coming."

"Oh, yes!" I shut my eyes. "Well, Uncle Hugo was very desperate. Alas, alas, what to do? He had no way to make a smoke signal. He had no flashlight to make a light signal."

"No telephone or telegraph," Miss Carlman said.

"No." I shut my eyes tighter. "So he was sitting there, just waiting to die, when suddenly he saw something bobbing in the water. It was a bottle that he had kept in the boat to carry drinking water. But it was empty and dry, because Uncle Hugo had not intended to be out long and he had not taken drinking water. So Uncle Hugo wrote a note—"

"Just a minute, Rupert," Miss Carlman said. "Where did he get the paper?"

"He wrote it on cloth," I said. "He tore some cloth from his shirt and dried it in the wind. He had his ball point pen in his pocket. So he wrote this note and put it in the bottle and corked it up tight and threw it out into the water."

"Yes, yes — go on!" said Miss Carlman.

"Well, there was a very big wind, and the bottle went bobbing along, merrily, merrily. Uncle Hugo watched it as long as he could see it and then he sat down to wait. He hoped and prayed that the bottle would keep going until it reached the shore. He hoped and prayed that it would not drift into some cattails, and stay there. He hoped and prayed that some smart people would find it and would come to rescue him."

I took a little rest.

"We are waiting," Miss Carlman said. "Just like Uncle Hugo."

"Well," I said, "it was a long, long time. About two hours. And then Uncle Hugo heard the put-put of a motorboat. It was like music to his ears."

"Is that what he said?"

"That's what he said. Uncle Hugo could see this motorboat cutting the waves, and it looked very good to him. He took off his shirt and waved it. On and on came the boat, headed straight for him. Sure enough, it had come to rescue him. 'Ahoy!' cried Uncle Hugo. 'Ahoy! Ahoy!'"

Right then, someone laughed. It was Miss Carlman.

"Honestly, Rupert," she said, "I must say you have a fine imagination! You have worked very hard to prove that a message in a bottle is a means of communication. You made up a very good story."

"Oh, he didn't make it up, Miss Carlman," Clayte said. "It's true."

Miss Carlman stared at Clayte. "Two of you — in the same class?" she said.

Old Milt reached in his pocket. "Here is the note," he said. He put it on the desk.

I think Miss Carlman's teeth almost dropped out.

"Three of you!" she said. "And I thought I knew my class! Milton, where did you get this note?"

"From my cousin Jim," Milt said. "Miss Carlman, Rupert's Uncle Hugo was shipwrecked right out on Rocky Island in the bay, yesterday. He sent this message in a bottle and it washed up on the sand by Mr. Peterson's fish shanty. So Mr. Peterson and my cousin Jim went out and rescued him."

"That's right," Dood said. "It was on TV this morning. It will be in the *Gazette* tonight."

Miss Carlman looked and looked at the note. It was really a piece of my uncle's shirt, and it said: Grounded on rocky island. Come out and get me before I freeze stiff!

"Well," Miss Carlman said, "we live and learn. Let me borrow the note, and when I see Miss Amory I will show it to her and tell her this tale of the sea. I am sorry, Rupert, that I did not know it before."

"Oh, that is O.K.," I said. "That is only because you are a lady, and you were not listening around the 'No Dames' corner — like some people."

I did not mention any names.

Groundhog's Party

IT WAS never my idea, having a birthday party. Mom and my sister Gwen dreamed that one up and gave me the bad news at breakfast.

"Rupert Piper," Gwen said, "take your elbows off the table and please don't scrape that jam jar again! The jam is almost sliding off your toast now! Rupert! Honestly, your manners!"

"It isn't my manners," I said. "It is gravity. We studied about it at school. A little jam flowed over to the side, and old gravity was right there to pull it down."

"And old Rupert was right there to wipe it up on his finger and lap it up!" Gwen said. "Mother, we will simply have to begin to train him!"

"Let's see," Mom said. "Rupert has not had a nice birthday party since he was seven. It is about his turn."

"What will we have to eat?" I said.

"That is not important — now," Mom said. "First, you will invite your friends."

"I will tell all three of them this morning," I said. "There's Milt Morrissey, across the street. Wait a minute. I'll yell at him." I started fast toward the door.

But Gwen grabbed me. "Rupert, you come back here!" she said. "Sit down."

"We won't do it that way, Rupert," Mom said. "We will make a nice list."

"Why?" I said. "It's just Milt and Clayte Snow and Doodleberries Hall."

"All the boys," Mom said. "And the girls."

My teeth almost dropped out. "You mean Smart Annabelle and Beautiful Sylvia and Opal—"

"All the girls," Mom said.

Well, that spoiled everything. But Clayte was yelling at the back door, so I grabbed my cap and jacket and departed.

"O.K.," Clayte said when he saw me. "Who died?"

"It's worse," I said. "I have to give a party and invite all the girls."

"Guys too?"

"Sure."

"Well," Clayte said, "it could be worse. What are we having to eat?"

"Dear, dear ladies' food," I said. "We have to eat out of a dish, with a fork and spoon. We have to wipe our faces on our dainty napkins and say 'No, thank you,' if we are offered more."

Milt came up and Dood was with him. "When is your birthday?" Milt said. "I suppose it is the same as Lincoln's or Washington's."

"No."

"Valentine's Day?" Doodleberries guessed.

"No," I said. "I am very sorry to say it is February second."

Milt moaned. "That is Groundhog's Day!"

"I know it," I said.

It is the day the groundhog comes out of his hole. If he sees his shadow, he goes back, and we have six weeks of winter. If he does not see his shadow, he stays out, and spring is supposed to come.

"It is very sad to have your birthday on Groundhog's Day," Clayte said. "They don't even close the bank. You have my sympathy. Will it be chocolate ice cream?"

"Tough luck!" said Dood. "Groundhog's Day! I like chocolate too."

"Look, Rupert," Milt said. "A big party will ruin your life. Annabelle and the girls will find out your birthday is on Groundhog's Day. Everyone will say you are a little groundhog. You will have to give a little party — just for us guys that you can trust. You can have hot dogs and ice cream, and we will come and suffer with you."

So I went home to give Mom the facts. "Mom," I said, "I have a very shameful secret that everyone is going to find out. Oh, how I suffer!"

"Wait a minute, Rupert," Mom said. "Something tells me I had better be sitting down before you say more." She sat down beside the kitchen table. "Now, what about this shameful secret?"

"Well," I said, "how would you like to hear everyone laughing at your son because he is a little groundhog?"

"Well, they laugh at him because he is a little pig," Mom said. "If you touch those cookies again before you wash those hands — Rupert Piper, can you tell me what makes you act so awful?"

"It's this way," I said. "If I was born on Lincoln's birthday, I would have to live up to Abraham Lincoln. If I was born on Washington's birthday, I would live up to George Washington. But I was born on Groundhog's Day, so I do not have much to live up to."

"Rupert Piper, wash those hands!"

I was mad. "O.K., Mom," I said. "I can wash away that little bit of clean bicycle grease, but I cannot wash away my birthday. It is on the calendar, for ever and ever, with a picture of a whiskery groundhog on it. How do you suppose I feel, alongside of Washington and Lincoln?"

"What," Mom said, "is this leading up to?"

"Mom, do I have to invite old Opal and old Annabelle—"

"Rupert!"

"Excuse me," I said. "I mean I cannot invite glamorous girls like Annabelle and Opal and Sylvia to a groundhog's party. How would they feel?"

"H'm!" Mom said. She smiled. "Rupert, the party will be on the Saturday before your birthday. Tomorrow you are to take the list to school and invi*e everyone in your room and check those who can come."

I would rather be dead three times but I did not say so.

"I have very poor groundhog manners," I said. "I do not know what to say."

"I have written this lovely little speech," Gwen said. "Read it to me, Rupert."

The speech said: "I am having a birthday party at two o'clock on Saturday afternoon. I wish all my dear friends to celebrate with me. Please come, since my happiness will be imcomplete without you."

So in the morning I read it to Milt and Clayte and Dood. "I am trapped," I said. "How I suffer!"

"You are too shy," Clayte said. "Rupert, tell your father to ask Annabelle's father if Annabelle can come, and to ask all the fathers if their dear, dear daughters can come."

"But," I said, "my dad will forget. And the girls' fathers will forget to tell them."

Milt puckered up his mouth and nodded his head. "Yes," he said, "that's what I had in mind."

So it snowed, and Dad was out cleaning the walks, and I went to help him.

"Dad," I said, "I am going to have a party, Saturday."

"Fine," he said. "Fine. Cuff it right into the street, Son."

"I have got to invite girls," I said.

"Girls, eh?"

"I am very shy with girls, Dad."

"Shy?" Dad said. "I thought I saw three girls walking with you today."

"They were behind me," I said. "A little behind me. Dad, will you take this little list and ask these girls' dads if these girls can come to my party?"

"Sure," Dad said. "Sure thing! Give it to me!"

So I took Mom's list and checked all the names because Dad had promised. "Here is the list, Mom," I said. "All checked."

"Well!" Gwen said. "You must be a very popular boy. Every girl said yes!"

So Saturday came, and Mom had the house all cleaned. She had sandwiches and ice cream and cake all ready. Gwen had some sweet little games planned, and there were some dear little prizes for the games.

I had to take two baths because Gwen looked at the first water, and there was not enough soap in it to suit her. I got dressed in my good suit and my white shirt with the blue cuff links.

"Rupert," Mom said, "you will stand at the door and greet your guests as they arrive and thank them for the presents."

"The presents?" I squeaked. *"Presents?"*

"It is your birthday party, isn't it?"

I guess I turned pale because the only guys I had invited were Milt and Clayte and Dood. I was sure Dad had forgotten to give the invitations to the girls' dads, and even if he remembered, I was sure their dads would forget. I would have only three presents!

The doorbell was ringing. "That will be Milt," I said.

"That is just some groceries," Mom said. "It is almost an hour before your guests will arrive."

"Then I am going somewhere," I said.

So I ran to Annabelle's house. Annabelle came to the door with some curlers on her hair.

"Annabelle," I said, "I am having a birthday party at two o'clock."

"How lovely!" said Annabelle.

"I wish all my dear friends to celebrate with me," I said.

Annabelle giggled. "Oh, Rupert! How cute!"

"I have to read this speech to every girl in class," I said.

"Oh, do continue!" said Annabelle. "Please!"

I continued. "Will you please come, since my happiness will be incomplete without you?"

"Oh, Rupert, I'd simply love to come!" Annabelle said. She flipped her eyelashes at me.

"O.K.," I said. "I'm taking presents at the door, and girls have got to be partners with girls in the games. See you!"

I went to Sylvia's house and made my speech, and then I went to Opal's. Opal was all dressed up.

"Where you going?" I said.

"Why, Rupert Piper!" Opal said through her nose. "I'm coming to your party!"

"Who invited you?" I said.

"Why, your mother, of course. She invited everyone in class! I will walk with you."

Was my face red! "Oh, no!" I said. "Oh, no, Opal, that isn't manners. I have to be at the door when you arrive — to take your present."

I had a very keen party with lots of presents and ice cream and hot dogs too. And the guys decided to be partners with the girls in the games — just this once.

Hobby Show

I GUESS you couldn't blame Miss Carlman. She only asked who had an idea for Friday afternoon, and up went Smart Annabelle's hand.

"Yes, Annabelle?"

"Miss Carlman, couldn't we have a hobby show, with everybody bringing their hobbies for our mothers to see?"

Beautiful Sylvia waved her hand as if she were flagging down a train. "Couldn't we have three judges and some prizes?"

Behind me Clayte moaned. I moaned back.

"Clayton Snow and Rupert Piper — quiet!" said Miss Carlman. "I think a hobby show is a splendid idea."

The guys met down in the "No Dames" corner of the playground. We were very gloomy. "I can see it

16

now!" said Milt. "The room all mussed up with Anna-belle's knitting."

"And Sylvia's exquisite little dolls," groaned Doodle-berries, "with a flock of ladies clucking around over them."

"Swell chance Limburger has of getting a prize!" said Milt. Limburger is Milt's hobby—a very keen white rat with pink popeyes. "They wouldn't like my electric stuff either," Milt said.

"Or my stamp collection," said Doodleberries.

"What're you bringing, Piper?" Clayte asked me.

I was very sad. I had quit rocks to take up camera, but films cost money. "I got a picture of the bloodmobile yesterday, on Main Street," I said.

Clayte shook his head. "The judges won't be inter-ested, and it will be thumbs down on my bug collection. Dames don't appreciate bugs."

Just as the bell rang, we got the keen idea. For once, we ran. We were in our seats before the girls. I raised my hand. "Miss Carlman, could we have some men for judges for our hobby show?"

"Men?" said Miss Carlman. "Well, that's a very good idea, Rupert, but you know men are working in the afternoon, so I guess we'll have to settle for ladies. Ladies will be very fair, I'm sure."

Smart Annabelle flipped her eyelashes at me. She thought the guys were outsmarted.

But after school Clayte said, "I've got an idea." He glanced all around. No one was trying to listen in but Opal, and Opal never knows the score. Clayte winked. "Let's all bring hobbies that ladies like. You know, I knit those mittens."

"That's right," said Milt. He grinned. "I can make a cake."

I said: "I'll take some very sweet, adorable, little sissy pictures. I have a film with just one exposure gone — that shot of the bloodmobile."

Smart Annabelle and Beautiful Sylvia spent half their time trying to find out what we were bringing. They even tried to look as if they were walking home with us.

"I'm bringing my crocheting," Annabelle said. "I've started a tablecloth. It's going to take five years. I'll be seventeen when it's finished! Just think — seventeen!"

"How perfectly thrilling!" said Sylvia. "I'm bringing my doll collection."

I moaned.

"I'm baking an apple pie," said Opal. "Then I'm going to take it home for supper. Grandpa's coming."

"I heard your grandpa had been decorated for bravery," said Milt. "Now I believe it!"

"Oh, it's true!" said Opal, through her nose. "In World War I."

A joke is wasted on Opal.

"I hope we'll have some very good boys' hobbies, for variety," said Annabelle. "What are you bringing, Rupert?"

"A surprise," I said.

Just then I noticed something gleaming in the gutter — someone's keys. I hustled right over to the police-station and waited for Chief Fox to finish his conversation with Bob Quillon, the photographer from the *Gazette*. Chief Fox was worrying his head off about a hit-and-run accident on the edge of town the day before.

"Blaine Smith's truck was parked off the highway, with a trailer full of chickens. Someone socked it from behind. Besides damaging the car, the crate flew open and the chickens got away! It happened plunk at four o'clock, because the car's clock stopped at four. Blaine says it was set by the mill whistle."

"Any clues?" Bob asked.

"Well, we've got an eye witness who says the runaway driver was Bill Warwick. But, Bill says he was right in town at four, parked at the entrance of the alley beside Pecks' grocery. He says the mill whistle blew while he sat there, and that he set his watch by it and checked with the courthouse clock."

"Who's your eye witness?" Bob asked.

"Flutey Harper."

"Flutey? I'd just take Bill's word!"

"I'd like to. If Bill only had a witness!" Chief Fox looked at me. "What'll it be, Rupert?"

I turned in the keys and explained. Chief Fox thanked me and said he'd let me know who owned them.

Then I went home and started working on my hobby. I had a little trouble, but I got a roll of pictures and developed them. I didn't have very keen subjects, but I gave them very important-sounding names.

Friday noon I took them to school. Everyone was busy arranging exhibits. I threw the picture of the bloodmobile in the wastebasket. It was crooked, and anyway it strictly wasn't for lady judges.

Miss Carlman walked around, looking surprised. "I

thought I knew my class," she told Miss Rockletter, the principal, when she came inspecting. "But this hobby show is revealing talents I hadn't dreamed of! See this beautiful little chocolate cake? Milton made it. Clayton knitted these mittens. Trowbridge raised this lovely geranium, and Rupert took these beautiful pictures."

" 'Rib Mountain'!" exclaimed Miss Rockletter. "What — er — unusual treatment!"

"See his 'Desert Cactus.' "

"Oh, yes," said Miss Rockletter. "The Pipers took a trip. Such detail!"

Annabelle was snooping around. I saw her reach into the wastebasket. "Oh, here's one of Rupert's adorable pictures!" she said. "Why, it's Main Street! Rupert, why did you throw away this perfectly marvelous picture?"

"I don't want it," I said.

"Oh, but Rupert!" said Miss Carlman. "We want this show to be a success! We need this picture for local color. Put it right here, Annabelle!"

Annabelle gave me a smarty look. The picture was cockeyed, and she knew it.

I was going to sound off, but two mothers had arrived, mine and Clayte's. Next, Mrs. Pipgrass and Miss Smithwick, two of the judges for the hobby show, entered.

"We have bad news, Miss Carlman," Mrs. Pipgrass said. "Mrs. Barcome can't make it!"

"Oh! Well, we'll ask another lady to judge."

The door opened and there stood Chief Fox. "I stopped about those keys, Rupert. They're Mr. Warner's. He sent you a dollar. Hey, what's going on here?"

"Oh Chief Fox!" Miss Carlman exclaimed. "Won't you help judge our hobby show? The boys wanted a man-judge, and—"

"Haven't a minute! Er—" The chief swallowed. He seemed to be looking at Milt's cake. He smiled, a kind of dreamy smile. "Do the judges sample the — er — hobbies?"

"Why, certainly, if they wish."

"Well, I guess I can take a little while off. My — er — duty, as a public servant."

Fine thing! A very revolting situation for the guys! We'd made a blunder. Chief Fox was going to have a fine opinion of guys who could knit and bake and raise geraniums. Maybe he'd fire us as police boys! Fine thing!

Well, the judges were Mrs. Pipgrass, Miss Smithwick, and Chief Fox. The first hobby looked at was Annabelle's five-year project. "Just think!" said Miss Smithwick. "This is going to take five years! Don't you look forward to seeing it finished?"

"If I last that long," said Chief Fox. "What with hit-and-run drivers. What is it?"

"A tablecloth," said Miss Carlman.

"To eat on? I'd hate to have to wait five years for my dinner. Haw! Haw!"

The ladies laughed very politely at the joke.

Chief Fox pointed at Milt's hobby. "That a cake?"

"Yes," said Miss Carlman. "Would the judges care to sample it?"

"Dear!" said Mrs. Pipgrass, with a queer look at the cake. "I'm on a diet."

"I'll take some," said Chief Fox.

We watched him eat it. He looked very pleased. "I'll take some more," he said.

The ladies discussed geraniums, then began making a disgusting fuss over the dolls.

"Oh!" smiled Miss Smithwick. "See these lovely flaxen braids!"

"This little girl has been collecting since she was four!" said Mrs. Pipgrass.

"Quite a while," said Chief Fox. He went and got another piece of Milt's cake.

Well, they got to my pictures at last. "This boy's hobby is photography," Miss Carlman said. "He took a trip last summer and certainly made the most of it."

Mrs. Pipgrass inspected the first photograph. "Rib Mountain!" she said.

I glanced over at my mother. She looked forever astonished. I felt kind of choked.

"And this," said Miss Carlman, "is a desert cactus."

Mother walked over. She examined my photos. "I guess I'll have to clear up a matter," she said. "This is a close-up of my little potted cactus, isn't it, Rupert?"

"Yes'm." I believe in telling the truth.

"H'm!" Chief Fox peered. "H'm! You don't say."

I got ready to turn in my police-boy badge.

"And Rib Mountain," Mother said, "is one of my raisin puddings, I believe, with cream on top."

"Why, Rupert!" Mrs. Pipgrass said. All the ladies laughed. Chief Fox looked at the picture.

"Pudding! My mother used to make 'em like that." He licked his lips.

Clayte poked me. "We've got a chance."

But the chief had picked up the next photo. "What's this?" he said, in a very sharp voice. "Who took this?"

"Rupert Piper," said Miss Carlman.

Chief Fox stuck the picture in front of my face. Piper?"

"Yes, sir." I guessed this was it!

Chief Fox stuck the picture in front of my face. "You take this?" he said.

"Yes, sir. It's not very good."

He pointed. "What's that?"

"The bloodmobile. I mean, that's what I tried to shoot."

"Then you took this Monday — the afternoon the bloodmobile was here?"

"Yes, sir. But I got it kind of cockeyed, and, well, I got Pecks' grocery, and the courthouse clock, and only half of the bloodmobile—"

"And this car in the alley, with the license number H19-304, and the courthouse clock at exactly four, just as Bill Warwick says!" He looked at Miss Carlman. "I'm taking this along. Good-by."

"But you didn't vote, Chief Fox!" said Mrs. Pipgrass.

"Oh! I vote for the cake—" He looked over where Milt's cake had been. "That hobby I ate up. I vote for that. Give that the girls' prize."

Milt's face was red as a neon sign.

"And give this picture the boys' prize!" Chief Fox gave me a salute. "See you later, Rupert. Thanks!" He was gone.

The ladies went into a huddle. Sylvia's dolls got the girls' prize, and Milt's late-lamented cake got the guys' prize.

Just then in walked Bob Quillon, from the *Gazette*, with his camera.

"Oh, are you going to photograph the prize winners?" Miss Carlman asked.

"Or the judges?" said Mrs. Pipgrass, winking.

"First, I came to get a shot of a photographer," Bob said. "Rupert Piper. His shot of Main Street solved a mystery."

"Oh Rupert!" said Annabelle. "Isn't it wonderful? You're a hero!"

I could feel the guys grinning. I wished I was a dead hero. I would rather be dead three times than do the disgusting, honest thing I had to do.

"Annabelle saved that picture," I said. "I threw it away."

"Fine, fine!" said Bob. "A shot of you and Annabelle then. Right here, please. Hold your camera, Rupert. Smile!"

Annabelle smiled. Not me.

So there was a big story in the *Gazette*. Sixth-grade hobby show solves hit-run mystery — Warwick absolved — Flutey Harper admits bumping chicken trailer—

Also, I'm sorry to say, there was a picture of Smart Annabelle, wearing her perfectly darling smile, and me, looking very tough. That was just to let the guys know they would have to settle with Rupert Piper for all smart cracks.

The Valentine Box

I T WAS a very cold, blowy morning, and the girls
walked to school in a huddle, with their arms around
each other, to keep warm.

Smart Annabelle and Beautiful Sylvia and Opal were
walking ahead of us.

Donna Darling was walking alone, reading her letter.

"A fine thing!" said Doodleberries. "Why do they
leave one girl out in the cold?"

"Maybe it is because Donna is new and they do not
know her very well," Clayte said. "What do you
think, Rupert?"

"Well," I said, "maybe it is because they do not like
her. If so, it is very unkind, and we will have to speak
to them about it. You are the best speaker, Milt."

26

"A very good idea," said Milt. "Also, it's very dangerous. My dad says no man should mix in a ladies' fight unless he can run."

"Walk a little slower, guys," I said. "We do not know Donna very well, either. Also, we do not wish her to think we are reading her letter over her shoulder, which would be very impolite."

So the bell rang, and Miss Carlman said, "Has everybody noticed what day is coming soon?" She pointed to the 14th of February, on the calendar. There was a heart on it, and a little Cupid with a bow and arrow, although bows and arrows are not allowed in our town.

"Everyone feels happy when Valentine's Day comes," Miss Carlman said. "Although the snow is cold and deep, it is spring in our hearts."

This sounded very mushy and Milt moaned, but Miss Carlman did not hear.

Annabelle was waving. "Miss Carlman," she said, "may we please have a valentine box?"

We knew this was coming, but Miss Carlman looked surprised. "Oh, what a lovely idea!" she said. "How many would like a valentine box?"

The girls raised their right hands. "Fourteen!" Miss Carlman said. "How many would not?"

All the guys raised their right hands. Also, their left hands. "Twenty-six!" Miss Carlman said. "Rupert Piper, what is one half of twenty-six?"

"Eighteen!" I said.

Everyone laughed, even Miss Carlman. "Rupert," she said, "I would have to give you zero in arithmetic today, only I know this is a joke. So I appoint you and Milton to bring the box. The girls will decorate it."

After school the girls tried to walk home with us, and we knew why.

"It is warmer this afternoon," Opal said. She covered her ears with her mittens, to keep them from freezing. "I feel as if it were spring."

"That's because Valentine's Day is coming," Annabelle said. She wasted a smile on me. "Valentines are a simply lovely way to let your friends know that you like them. If people are too shy to say it right out, they can put all their lovely thoughts in a valentine."

"Well," Milt said, "I am not too shy to say my lovely thoughts right out.

> Roses are red,
> Violets are blue,
> Lemons are sour,
> And so are you!

Milt jumped up in the air, and whooped.

"Oh, Milty," Opal said, "you're so cute!" Opal does not always know the score. "I am going to send a valentine to everyone in our room — except one, she said.

"So am I," said Annabelle and Sylvia.

Clayte poked me. He said, "You know what they mean."

"I sure do," I said. "They mean Donna."

"On guard, Rupert!" Dood whispered.

Annabelle was sneaking up on us. "Rupert," she said, "are you going to make your valentines, or buy them?"

"A very good question," I said. "Now I will ask you one. How come you girls leave Donna out of everything?"

"Donna Darling?" Sylvia said. "Why, we don't!"

"We've got eyes," Milt said. "Every day we see you playing ring-tag, and we see Donna all alone, reading something."

"Donna does not care to play with us," Annabelle said. "There is a girl in her home town who was her best friend, since kindergarten. Her name is Gloria. Gloria writes to Donna every day, and Donna writes to her every day. They are going to visit each other, next summer. Donna did not want to move here, and she does not want new friends."

"A very long answer," I said. "Also, a queer one!"

The next day we were rolling big snowballs to make a fort. Clayte said, "There is Donna, standing alone in the sunshine, reading her letter."

"She looks very unhappy," Milt said. "I am sorry to say it is up to someone to go and talk to her."

"O.K.," I said. "I, Rupert Piper, will do this deed of mercy."

Milt shook my hand. "Rupert," he said, "if you do this good deed, I will be right there — a little behind you."

"So will I," said Clayte and Doodleberries.

"Let us not delay," said Clayte. "Let us not stand here talking about it a long time."

"Guys who talk about the good deeds they are going to do, never get them done," said Dood. He sat down on his snowball. "We will only talk about it a little while."

Clayte sat down, too. He said, "We do not wish to scare Donna, or sneak up on her."

"Or jump out at her," I said. "After all, she does not

know us very well. What will we talk to her about?"

Milt was making a very soft snowball. "I know," said Milt. "We will apologize. Girls love people who apologize."

I said, "What will we apologize for?"

"For this!" said Milt. He threw the soft snowball at Donna. It hit her letter, and broke up, and fell at her feet.

Donna looked very surprised. She began to shake the snow off the letter, and wipe the letter on her coat — but she was looking at us.

"Hep! Hep! Forward march!" said Milt.

As we marched up, Donna stuffed the letter in her pocket and grabbed some snow.

"Look, Donna," Milt said. "I — Ouch!"

Donna's snowball smacked him right against his nose.

"Hey!" Clayte said. "We only came to — Hey!" A snowball landed in his stomach, and another went down Dood's neck.

Milt grabbed Donna's arm. "Donna, I wish to tell you — oops!" Milt was flat on his face, telling it to the snow.

When he sat up, Donna was running away, and Annabelle and Sylvia were walking past.

Annabelle flipped her eyelashes at him. "How is the snow today?" she said.

"Look," Milt said, "my legs felt a little tired, so I flopped down."

"Well," Sylvia said, "it might be that. Or it might be that someone threw you down."

"Someone like Donna," Annabelle said.

So we knew they saw. They walked away, giggling.

"O.K.," Milt said. "Just for that, I will not apologize. Rupert, your good deed backfired."

"Right!" I said. "I will not do any more good deeds for Donna. Let her get all her valentines from her old friend, Gloria, too!"

We were saving box tops, to get an outer-space map and binoculars, so we mailed them in on Monday.

On Tuesday we went to the post office to see if there was a package for us. Donna came in and mailed a letter, and asked the postmaster if there was one for her.

We went on Wednesday and Thursday and Friday and Saturday and Monday. Every day Donna came in and mailed a letter and asked for one.

At recess she stood around alone, reading her letter.

Milt said, "When I see something, I see something, and I do not need space binoculars to see it. Donna reads the same letter, every day."

"That's right," I said. "It is the same letter she was reading the day she threw you — excuse me! It's the same letter that got hit by your snowball. The ink is all runny."

Clayte said, "Every morning the postmaster tells her no, there is no mail."

"She was almost crying this morning," I said. "If I liked girls, I would write her a letter."

"Well," Dood said, "we can write one, anyway. What can we say?"

Milt said, "We can apologize."

"Why?" said Dood. "She threw a snowball down my neck."

"Right," said Milt. "But I have been thinking. If I moved away, you guys would promise to write a letter every day. So maybe I would not make new friends. I would just wait for your letters. Dood would write one, Tuesday. On Wednesday, you would sit in the 'No Dames' corner and tell each other that old Milt Morrissey was a very good guy, and you missed him. Then Opal would come along and you would chase her, and forget all about me. So I would go to the post office every day and the postmaster would tell me, 'No letter!' "

"Take a breath, Milt," Dood said. "You are blue in the face."

"I will go on," I said. "I will be the boy who moved away. Then, some day, I would be reading my old letter from Dood, and sock! one of the new guys would hit me with a snowball. I would hit right back and trip one fellow and throw him in the snow, and—"

"Look out, Rupert!" Milt said.

"I will take over," Clayte said. "I will be the guy who moved. Well, no letter would come, and no one would play with me, and I would wish I was dead three times. So — I would buy valentines for all the new guys and girls—"

"Wait a minute!" Dood said. "If you saw Donna buying valentines, they were just for her dear, dear old friends at home."

"Then she mailed them in the wrong box," Clayte said. "She stuffed them all in our valentine box, this morning."

My teeth almost dropped out. "Well," I said, "she is not getting any from us."

"Right!" said Milt. "And you know what the girls said. They are sending valentines to everyone in the class — except one."

I took out my wallet. I said, "I'm doing another good deed."

"So am I," said the guys. "And this time we will not stop to talk about it."

So we had the valentine box, and Milt and Annabelle called the names. There were twenty-eight present and everyone had at least twenty-seven valentines, and so did Donna.

"How come?" I said to Smart Annabelle. "You said you were going to send valentines to everyone — except one. Who is the one?"

"Why, me!" Annabelle said. "Naturally, we didn't send to ourselves. Honestly, Rupert! Didn't you know it was a joke?"

"Oh, sure!" I said. "Sure!"

The guys put their valentines in their geography books.

But the girls put theirs on their desks and took turns admiring them.

"This one from you is simply darling, Donna," Annabelle said. She put her arm around Donna.

"The one you sent me is adorable!" Donna said.

And then all the girls stood in a huddle looking at the valentines they got from the boys, and whispering about them, and wasting smiles on us.

Two, If By Sea

ALTHOUGH Valentine's Day was two months past, the girls kept wasting smiles on us. But we had other troubles, so we hardly noticed them.

We were all very worried and nervous about a friend of ours who is a mule named Aunt Dottie. We wondered if Reginald Whipple would tease her, while we were in school.

This Reginald was visiting his grandpa in town, while his school had spring vacation. On Saturday he came over to the sandlot, all dressed up.

Clayte invited him to play ball.

"No, thanks," Reginald said. "I'll watch. I find your childish sports amusing."

Well, that was not polite. So Milt said, "What kind of pants are those?"

"I ride a horse," Reginald said. "Grandfather gave me a very fine horse, named Featherstone. These are my riding pants, naturally. And yours?"

"These are my riding pants, naturally," Milt said. "Also, they are my walking pants and my working pants. They are my pants, period."

Aunt Dottie was over in the corner of the lot, eating a few dandelions. Reginald gave her a very mean look. He said, "Maybe you fellows don't know what a horse is."

"Please tell us," said Dood.

"Yes," I said. "What is a horse, Reginald?"

"Well," Reginald said, "well, — a horse is just a horse. That's a silly question. I refuse to answer."

"I will tell you, Rupert," Milt said. "A horse is a short-eared mule."

This was a joke and everyone laughed except Reginald.

"I am wasting my time," he said. He picked up an old candy bag, blew it up and popped it loudly in Aunt Dottie's ear.

Aunt Dottie yawned. She had been in the army, and she was used to big guns.

So Reginald picked up a stick, and I yelled, "Easy, boy! You tease Aunt Dottie at your own risk!"

"Hah!" Reginald said. "Who's afraid of a mule? You are talking to a man who personally won three ribbons, riding a very spirited horse."

"Well," I said, "you are talking to a man who once personally teased Aunt Dottie with a popsickle, and is very surprised to be alive to tell it. But if you wish to learn the hard way, go ahead."

Just then Smart Annabelle and Beautiful Sylvia and Opal came along, going to their twirling lesson.

"Oh, we just heard the most wonderful news!" Annabelle said. "We are going to celebrate Paul Revere Day!"

"Very wonderful!" I said. "Dood, you're next batter."

"The Historical Society thought it up," said Sylvia. "Mrs. Peterkin is president, so Mayor Peterkin is in on it, too!"

"The poor man!" I said. "Strike one!"

"It will be a big pageant," Annabelle said, "to act out Paul Revere's ride."

"Hah!" said Reginald. "You can't do that, in this town."

"We can, too," said Opal. "This is a very patriotic town. Milty is named for Paul Revere. Milton Paul Revere Morrissey."

Well, that is so. Milt's birthday is April 18th, and that is the anniversary of Paul Revere's ride. Milt's grandfather gave him five dollars, once, to memorize Mr. Longfellow's poem about it.

But we were very busy and we did not think about the Paul Revere celebration until Monday. Then Mrs. Peterkin came to school to tell us about it.

"We are going to divide our town," she said. "One street will be named Medford. One will be named Lexington, and one Concord. Mr. Longfellow's beautiful poem will be read over a very powerful sound system, so that it can be heard all over town. There will be

sound effects too, and spotlights on the actors. There
will be parts for everyone."

Milt waved. "Mrs. Peterkin," he said, "what will we
use for a church tower?"

"A very good question," said Mrs. Peterkin. "Paul
Revere's friend will climb the tower of the North
Avenue Church, and place the lanterns aloft. 'One, if
by land, and two, if by sea.' Remember? Paul Revere
will be waiting at the bridge to start his ride. Questions?"

The guys had a big question. Clayte poked me. "Ask
Miss Carlman, Rupert," he said. "Go ahead. I'll be
hiding right behind you!"

"Miss Carlman," I said. "I am not asking this for
myself. I would not be so selfish. I am asking it for
some poor hungry friends, who get very hungry out in
the fresh air. I mean, I will eat a very good supper
on pageant night and place a few spare olives in my
pocket, and have only a few bad hunger pains and
some little ones, but—"

Annabelle waved. "Miss Carlman," she said, "Rupert
is working up the courage to ask if there will be anything to eat. But some people are not always thinking
of their stomachs when Mr. Longfellow's beautiful
poem is going to be acted out — so the girls wish to
know who is going to be Paul Revere."

Mrs. Peterkin answered. "Well," she said, "well
— you see, Paul must have a horse and ride it, so Rupert's question is easier. After the pageant, there will
be a parade to Legion Hall, and there will be coffee
or cocoa and doughnuts for everyone."

Opal raised her hand. "Mrs. Peterkin," she said,

"there is one boy who should really be Paul Revere, and—"

"We know that, dear," said Mrs. Peterkin. "And we are going to ask him. I do hope he will consent!"

So all the guys grinned at Milt, and after school we went home with him, to help him with his problem.

Milt's dad was in the kitchen having early supper, as it was bowling night.

"Well, Dad," Milt said, "your great patriotism really pays off! You named me Paul Revere, and now I am happy to tell you that you will have to buy me a horse."

"A horse!" Milt's mom almost dropped her cup. "A horse, to eat us out of house and home? What put that in your head?"

"Patriotism!" Milt said. "On my birthday, the people 'will waken and listen to hear the hurrying hoofbeats of that steed'—"

"I get it!" Milt's dad said. "I heard about the celebration. Have they asked you?"

"Not yet," Milt said. "But Mrs. Peterkin said there was one man for the job, so—"

Milt's mom and dad looked at each other. "Milton," his mom said, "I would not make plans, dear."

"But — Mom!" Milt said. "My name is M. Paul Revere Morrissey, and—"

"I know," his mom said. "But sometimes people have to consider other matters."

"Well, if I'm asked, can we rent a horse?" Milt said.

They looked at each other again. His dad said, "If you're asked."

Walking to school next morning, Clayte said, "Who else can they ask?"

Reginald was walking part way with us. "Hah!" he said. "What would you ride, Morrissey? A broomstick? Or, maybe, that mule?"

"I'll get along," Milt said.

Reginald laughed a very horrible laugh, and went into the store.

Dood said, "I hope he spends his next vacation at the South Pole."

That day Mrs. Peterkin announced the pageant actors. First, she named the farmers and redcoats and farmers' wives and the singers. Clayte was a shopkeeper, in Lexington.

Then Mrs. Peterkin said, "Trowbridge Hall will be Paul Revere's friend who climbs the tower. Also, Paul will have two nameless assistants, who hold his horse while he mounts it. They are Rupert Piper and Milton Morrissey."

I hoped I was dreaming, but I was not. Poor old Milt put on a big smile, but he did not mean it.

Opal waved. "Mrs. Peterkin," she said, "did you know that Milton Paul Revere Morrissey's birthday is the 18th of April?"

"O-o-oh! How interesting!" said Mrs. Peterkin. "Then, Milton, you'll feel honored indeed to be Reginald's assistant."

My teeth almost dropped out.

"Reginald?" Milt said. His voice squeaked. "Reginald is Paul Revere?"

"Yes," Mrs. Peterkin said. "Isn't it lovely? He rides beautifully, and has his own horse. And isn't he kind to consent?"

Very kind. Hah!

At recess, Milt said, "I guess I will not be in the pageant."

"But, Milton," Annabelle said, "you are still Milton Paul Revere Morrissey!"

"You are still patriotic," Opal said.

Sylvia said, "You must take the part, for Paul Revere's sake."

"That is so," Milt said. "Well, O.K. I guess I can stand down at the bridge with Reginald — and listen to him brag — for Paul's sake."

"Me, too," I said.

On pageant night Reginald and Milt and Dood and I waited on North Avenue. We were dressed alike in colonial costumes, with some hair in a braid behind us.

Reginald said, "Look at the people on the streets! This is going to be some horse show!"

"Well," Milt said, "that was not what Paul Revere had in mind, but maybe he did not have as fine a horse as Featherstone."

Featherstone was tied down beside the bridge.

The pageant started with some music. Then some gun salutes were fired.

"What's the idea?" Reginald said. "Those guns will scare Featherstone."

In a minute the reading began, over the sound system.

"Listen, my children, and you shall hear,
Of the midnight ride of Paul Revere,
On the eighteenth of April, in Seventy-five . . ."

The spotlight turned on us. Reginald pretended to talk to Dood, while the reader went on.

"He said to his friend, 'If the British march
By land or sea from the town tonight
Hang a lantern aloft in the belfry arch
Of the North Church tower as a signal light,
One, if by land, and two, if by sea . . .'"

When this was over, the spotlight left us and shone on a boat that Bob Quillon was rowing across the river. Bob was in a colonial costume, and he looked like Paul Revere.

While he was rowing, we ran across the bridge in the dark. The spotlight shone on the coal boat, as the reader read about the British warship, named the *Somerset*.

By this time, we have reached Featherstone. Featherstone was acting queer. He was snorting and jumping around.

"What ails him?" I said.

"I told you," Reginald said. "He doesn't like guns. He'll be all right when we start the ride."

Milt said, "I'm supposed to hold him for you."

"Thanks, pal," said Reginald, "but you had better stick to mules."

"Well, that suits me," Milt said.

The spotlight was on Dood, who was very busy watching for the British.

Reginald untied Featherstone. Featherstone put up his nose and whinnied. The next minute he was away, galloping down the alley.

"Whoa! Whoa!" Reginald shouted, but Featherstone was out of sight.

"Stop!" Reginald yelled. "Stop the pageant!"

There was some loud music. No one heard him.

"Don't worry, Reginald," I said. "I will get a horse."

I ran as fast as I could down Walnut to Oak Street. Aunt Dottie was standing in her lot, half asleep. I jumped on her back. "The British are coming, Aunt Dottie!" I said. "Come on!"

Cloppety-clop, we ran to the bridge, and I slid off. "Here is Aunt Dottie, Reginald," I said. "The nation is saved!"

Reginald was so mad that he cried. "That long-eared mule! I will not disgrace myself!"

"Look, Reginald," Milt said. "Paul Revere was not thinking about what kind of ears his horse had. It was the fate of the nation that was important."

The spotlight turned on us. We could hear the reader.

"Booted and spurred, with a heavy stride
⠀On the opposite shore walked Paul Revere."

Reginald was stamping, but it was only because he was so mad.

Suddenly a light shone in the belfry of the church. Then a second light shone.

"That's it!" Milt said. "Get going, Reginald!"

Paul Revere was supposed to ride along the riverbank and up onto Washington Street, to where Medford began.

In a few minutes the big sound effects clock would be booming twelve. The crowd would be waiting —

and no Paul Revere! Reginald was standing just out of the spotlight, howling. The redcoats could come, for all he cared.

"It's up to you, Milt," I said. "For once, the girls were right. You are still patriotic. So make the ride — for Paul Revere's sake."

Milt hopped on Aunt Dottie's back. "Give it all you've got, Aunt Dottie," he said. "The British are coming!"

So Paul Revere was on time in Medford and in Lexington and in Concord. Maybe somebody laughed at his horse, but he got there.

Some more guns were fired, and I guess Feather-stone ran out of his skin, if he heard them.

At last the pageant was over, and all the actors met down at the end of Washington Street to start the parade.

Mayor Peterkin was there. "Mister Mayor," Milt said, "I guess you want Reginald to lead the parade, because he is the real Paul Revere."

Right then Mrs. Peterkin ran up and did a very embarrassing thing. She hugged poor old Milt and kissed him. Oh, the agony! Then she hugged me and Aunt Dottie, too, and she cried all over us.

She said, "You saved our pageant, just as Paul Revere saved the country, by seeing what to do and doing it bravely. Take your place at the head of the parade, Milton. We are proud of you."

Annabelle and Sylvia and Opal were standing there in colonial costumes, wasting smiles.

Milt is a very honest guy. He made a speech. "Well, the girls coaxed us to be in the pageant. They coaxed all the guys. We only did what was patriotic. We did not think of our stomachs, when Mr. Longfellow's beautiful poem was being acted out. But it is over now and — well, maybe Aunt Dottie is thinking of her stomach, a little."

"Oh, dear!" said Mrs. Peterkin. "There will be no treat for — er — Aunt Dorothy, at the Legion Hall party. It's only doughnuts."

"Very keen!" I said. "Very keen! Aunt Dottie learned to love doughnuts in the army."

Hard Luck Hank

WELL, the British came and the British went and so did Reginald Whipple. Which is a good thing, because in the spring we guys concentrate on baseball and we wouldn't even want Reginald for our water boy.

We Lincoln Lions were all ready for some very stiff baseball practice when a fellow wheeled up, parked his bike, and looked into the schoolyard.

"That looks like a Mayville Eagle," said Doodleberries. "He is out spying, to see if we are going to be hard to beat, when we play them next week."

The Eagle pulled up his belt and walked toward us. Milt poked me, "Watch this, Piper," he said.

Clayte said, "Oh, that is my dear cousin, Sandy

Clark. He's coming over to talk. Hey, Sandy! Why aren't you in school?"

"Teacher's conference," Sandy said. "We got out, this afternoon. I came over to warn you."

Some of our cheerleaders were walking past, namely, Smart Annabelle, Beautiful Sylvia, and Opal, giggling and bouncing their balls.

"I notice we have a few spies around this place," Clayte said. "Come over to our 'No Dames' corner, Sandy."

So we had a little talk in the "No Dames" corner. "One of our guys is going to move here," Sandy said. "His folks are going on a trip, and he is going to live with his aunt and go to your school. He will want to play on your baseball team, so I will tell you what to say. Be very firm. Say, 'The answer is no, and that is final, Hard Luck Hank.'"

"Hard Luck Hank?" Clayte said.

Sandy nodded. "That's the name for him. And luck is very important in baseball. With Henry Winkle on your team, you would lose every game. I would not care, if I did not have a cousin on your team."

I said, "Is Hank a good guy?"

"Oh, sure," Sandy said.

"Well," Milt said, "a fellow can't help his luck."

"No," Sandy said. "This guy can't. He is just awkward. He is awkward with his legs. When he kicks a ball, it goes crazy places. We stopped playing kickball at our school because of Hank's hard luck. He can't wrestle without spraining a thumb, or something."

"This is baseball," I said.

"Sure," Sandy said. "And when Hard Luck Hank

swings at a ball, I would hate to tell you what happens. We almost quit baseball, too, because of him and his horrible luck."

The bell rang.

"Well," Sandy said, "I just thought I'd tell you, because my cousin is on your team."

"Thanks," Clayte said.

When we were running in, Opal said, "What was Sandy Clark doing here?"

"How do you know him?" I said.

"He lives next door to my grandma in Mayville," Opal said. "My aunt is his teacher."

"Well," Clayte said, "my dear cousin came to tell the Lincoln Lions something. He did not send any messages to any cheerleaders."

Hank came to school on Monday. "We are very glad to have Henry Winkle for the rest of the year," Miss Carlman said. "Henry, what is your hobby?"

Henry is a fellow with a big grin and freckles. "Well," he said, "I like baseball. I expect I'll be on the team."

"That is lovely," Miss Carlman said. "You will be playing your old team on Friday. Do you think we will beat them?"

"Well," Henry said, "they are a hard team to beat, but maybe we will have good luck."

"You see," Miss Carlman said, "Henry is new in our school, but he is loyal."

So at recess we hurried to the "No Dames" corner. "If he is so loyal," Milt said, "he can lead the cheers. The girls would like a boy cheerleader."

The sixth-grade girls have green skirts and white

sweaters with a green "L" on them, and they cheer when we play games.

"Here comes Hank," Clayte said. "Remember what Sandy said. The answer is no, to Hard Luck Hank."

So Milt and I chose teams, but we did not choose Hank.

"Which team am I on?" he said. "Yours, Rupert?"

I did not like to say, "No, Hard Luck Hank, that is final."

So I said, "I guess I have enough men, Hank."

"Then I'm on Milt's team," Hank said.

"Sorry," Milt said, "I have enough on mine, today, too."

"Well," Hank said, "I'll be water boy and pinch hitter. If you need me, let me know. I will go practice batting."

He went down to the back of the schoolyard.

Smart Annabelle and Sylvia and Opal were listening in. "You boys are very unkind," said Sylvia.

"Hank is loyal," said Opal.

"Well," Dood said, "Hank has bad luck. He is known as Hard Luck Hank. We do not want to lose the game."

"It is better to lose a baseball game than to be impolite," said Annabelle.

"Well," I said, "no one would say that but a girl."

"Then I am very glad to be a girl," said Annabelle. "We are going down and bring the ball back to Henry when he bats it."

So they went away, and we practiced. But we did not have a very good game. We kept pitching wild, and no one could hit.

When the bell rang, Milt said, "I think some of

Hank's bad luck got around, anyway. We will have to do better than this, or we will not beat Mayville."

The girls were laughing when they ran in. "Did you have a good time?" Miss Carlman asked them.

Annabelle flipped her eyelashes at me. "We had a wonderful time," she said. "We ran miles and miles. It is very good exercise for cheerleaders."

Hank looked happy too.

"Henry," Miss Carlman said, "your teacher is coming to see me today. I am sure she will give me a very good report on you."

So after school, Milt had an idea. "Rupert," he said, "we have not been doing our manly duty. It is about time we helped clean erasers and wash blackboards.

"You are right, Milt," I said. "It is our manly duty."

So we stayed to help Annabelle and Sylvia and Opal and the girls. After a while, Hank's teacher came. She is Miss Duncan.

The blackboard was very dirty behind Miss Carlman's desk, so Milt and I washed it three times. We heard what was said, as we are not deaf.

Miss Carlman said, "Henry seems to be a very fine pupil."

"Very fine," Miss Duncan said. "But I am almost glad to get rid of him, for a while. He's a charming boy, but he does have the worst luck!"

I do not have long eyelashes, but I flipped them the best I could, at Annabelle.

Miss Duncan said, "The boys enjoy kickball, but due to Hank's hard luck our ball is now on top of the church on the corner, cuddled up tight against the base of the steeple. So near, and yet so far! And then," Miss Duncan said, "poor Henry had the hard luck to bat a baseball through Brenner's Grocery window."

Milt put his hand over his mouth and snickered.

"Boys," Miss Carlman said, "the board looks lovely. Please clean the erasers — outdoors."

So we went outside. "You see," I said, "Hank is really Hard Luck Hank."

Annabelle said, "Rupert Piper, do you know where Brenner's Grocery store is?"

"No," I said.

"Tell him, Opal," Sylvia said.

Opal said, "Brenner's Grocery store is half a block from Mayville School. The church is half a block from school. Do you have any one on our team who can bat a ball that far?"

That was all we had to know.

We invited Hank to a big meeting in the "No Dames" corner. "Hank," Milt said, "we are very honest guys. We are sorry we were not polite to a poor guy with bad luck, who can bat a ball half a block."

Hank grinned. "Oh, that's O.K."

So the Mayville Eagles came to play on Friday. "I notice Hard Luck Hank is water boy," Sandy said.

"You are very right," Milt said, and the game began.

The cheerleaders were very noisy, but it was a see-saw ball game.

In the first inning, Clayte struck out three Eagles. They made one hit. We did not happen to hit.

In the second inning, Mayville barely happened to make a home run, and the score was 1-0 in their favor, as we did not happen to hit.

In the third inning, Mayville had two men on base and two out when Clayte struck Sandy out. Dood's elegant home run evened the score.

Mayville managed to get in two runs in the fourth, so the score was 3-1 in their favor.

We got drinks from Hank, and evened it up in the fifth, at 3 and 3.

In the sixth, Sandy homered — the show-off. He happened to drive in another run. It was not our inning, and the score was 5 to 3.

I homered in the seventh. The Eagles stayed ahead, 5-4. We all had a drink of water, and Hank tried to say some cheerful words, like, "What's the matter with you guys? You play like you're asleep! You bat like poor old grandmothers! If you don't go to town in this next inning, you are sunk."

In the eighth, the Eagles scored one run, so they had a very small lead of 6 to 4, when Milt got up to bat.

Milt singled.

Clayte was next batter. He singled.

I was next. I singled.

Dood took the mound. Sandy put on a mean look, and struck him out.

Hard Luck Hank put the dipper in the pail and stood up and pulled his belt tight and walked over to the mound.

"Hey, wait!" Sandy yelled. "Is your water boy going to bat?"

"Well," I said, "it is the best we can do. Our next batter hurt his wrist a little, and Hank is our pinch hitter."

"Play ball!" yelled Opal.

So Sandy wound up and pitched.

Sock went Hank's bat! The ball zoomed straight over Sandy's head and over the heads of a few more players, and down to the back of the schoolyard.

Milt and Clayte and I got home, and so did Hank. The Lincoln Lions were ahead, 8 to 6. The girls were cheering.

Hank went back to his water pail and sat there and grinned. He was hard luck — to the Eagles. They did not score again.

We won, 10 to 6.

"Well," Sandy said, "I see you have made a player of Hard Luck Hank."

Annabelle and Opal and Sylvia were standing there. "Sure," Milt said, "the girls taught the poor guy to play."

"That's right," Hank said. "The Lincoln cheerleaders know a great deal about baseball."

The cheerleaders gave us some smiles and for once they were not wasted. We gave them a few, right back.

These Moms!

I FELT trouble in my bones when Miss Carlman announced, "Mother's Day is coming, and we want to do something special. Who has an idea?"

Milt waved first.

"Yes, Milton?"

Milt stood up and smiled. Milt is a smart guy with smart ideas. "Miss Carlman," he said, "what if our moms don't want any gifts? I asked my Mom what she wanted, and she said. 'Nothing! Please omit Mother's Day — I hope!'"

"Well!" said Miss Carlman. "That is certainly very strange! Did she explain?"

"Yes," Milt said. "She said the memory of the last burned toast was fresh in her mind. She said she hoped she had cleaned her last Mother's Day breakfast-in-bed off the kitchen ceiling."

This was a joke, so everyone laughed.

Miss Carlman said, "Well, since breakfast in bed is not very popular with some mothers, who has a better idea?"

Smart Annabelle waved. Clayte poked me. "Watch it, Piper. This will be worky."

"Yes, Annabelle?"

"Couldn't we have a party for all our mothers?" Annabelle said.

Sylvia waved. "Couldn't we all earn money for gifts and present them to our mothers at the party and tell how we earned the money?"

"That sounds like a very good idea," said Miss Carlman. "I shall talk to Miss Rockletter. Ready for recess."

The fellows hustled to the "No Dames" corner. Dood made a speech. "My Mom is O.K." he said, "Mother's Day is O.K. Giving my mother a gift is O.K. But letting the girls boss us around is not O.K. Also—"

"Also," I said, "we are broke."

"The girls will get all the jobs." said Milt. "And all the money. They will buy their mothers fancy gifts. We will give our mothers peanut gifts, and the girls will laugh at us."

"We will have to earn some money," Clayte said. "If we can't earn it easy, we will have to work."

"Mom," I said that night, "what can I do to help?"

"To — help?" Mom looked at me. "Rupert Piper, where do you hurt?"

"I don't hurt, Mom," I said. "I feel good and strong and worky, so I'd like some job to do."

"Have you a fever?" Mom said. "Come here!" She felt my forehead.

"What's the idea, Mom?" I said. "Just because a fellow wants to help. Shall I go to the grocery?"

"Well — yes," Mom said. "And since I didn't have to talk an hour and push you out the door, you may have thirty cents for yourself."

That was keen. So I went to the grocery.

When I was coming home past the vacant lot, something was wiggling around. I braked my bike and went to look. There was a funny-looking rabbit. I guessed someone had it for a pet and didn't like it because it looked funny.

"I guess someone kicked you out," I said. "I am Rupert Piper, and you're invited to spend the night with me."

I put him in my bike basket on top of the bag of corn meal. Then I remembered what Mom said once. "Rupert, the next time you bring home a stray dog or cat, I am going to take you both to the dog pound."

But this rabbit had very sad eyes, and I felt sorry for him. I had an extra paper bag in my bike basket so I pushed the rabbit into it, and put some clover in there with him, and went home.

When my sister Gwen was not looking, I took the rabbit up to my room. I put him in my closet and put the clover on the floor and shut the door.

When I went to bed, my rabbit was asleep. But in

the night I woke up, and he was scratching around, making lots of noise. I was glad my closet wasn't near anyone's room.

At breakfast, Gwen said, "I heard a funny noise in the night."

"So did I," I said. "Maybe a tree branch was scraping the porch."

"But I've got trouble," I told the fellows. "My rabbit won't eat."

"Buy him some grain," Milt said. "Mrs. Pipgrass has some rabbits in her basement and I saw her buying grain for them."

So the grain cost thirty cents, and I was broke.

"Mom," I said, "can I help, tonight? I'll do the dishes."

"You must be growing up," Mom said. "I'm tired and I'll pay you thirty cents."

The next night I earned sixty cents washing the back porch and walk, and I found a dime in my old blue jacket. So I had a dollar.

I was going to buy Mom's present in the morning, but then that C.O.D. package came.

"Oh, dear," Mom said. "I need another dollar and I don't have it! Everything happens when your father is out of town!"

"Rupert Piper is here, Ma," I said. "I can loan you a dollar."

So I was broke.

The next day Miss Carlman said: "Boys and girls, the Mother's Day party is tomorrow. Are you all prepared?"

"I have a dollar," Annabelle said. "I earned it baby-sitting."

"I have seventy cents," said Beautiful Sylvia. "I'm earning thirty tonight."

"I have two dollars!" said Opal through her nose. "I got them from Grandpa. I didn't do anything."

"But, Opal," Miss Carlman said. "You were to earn the money."

"I earned it," Opal said. "I went over to sing for Grandpa, and he said he'd give me two dollars — if I wouldn't sing!"

Everyone laughed, and Opal thought she was very funny.

Milt and Clayte and Dood hadn't counted their money. I said. "I have enough — if I get it back. I loaned it to someone."

Mom forgot to pay me back, and I hated to ask her. She forgot in the morning too, and it was party day. I felt awful.

Then I remembered my rabbit.

"Mom," I said, "are you coming to school today?"

"Oh, yes, Rupert. It's a special meeting."

The mothers didn't know it was a party. It was a surprise.

"Mom," I said, "there are different kinds of presents. I mean, there are cold presents and warm, furry presents."

"Give me the cold ones, every time," Mom said.

So I started over. "Mom," I said, "there are very silent presents like diamond bracelets and flowers and handkerchiefs, and then there are presents that make a lot of noise, scratching around in the night. They keep you company."

Mom laughed. "I hope you weren't considering a diamond bracelet," she said.

I felt better. I guessed I was talking her into it. "Oh, no," I said. "Don't you worry, Mom. I won't get you a cold something that just lies still in a box."

I put on my cap and went to the door. "Don't worry, Mom," I said. "Even if everybody else gets something that is no company, you will get something that can wiggle and hop around."

I shut the door and picked up my rabbit in the bag, and ran — because if I stayed, I couldn't keep the good news to myself much longer and I would surely tell Mom my secret.

All the moms came to school that afternoon. Miss Smithwick came too, and Mrs. Pipgrass. Mrs. Pipgrass had red eyes as if she had a cold or had been crying.

So we had the party. First we had a program. "And now," Miss Carlman said, "we have a surprise for you mothers. Each boy and girl has earned a Mother's Day gift."

My Mom's face turned very red, and I knew she was thinking about the dollar she forgot to pay back. I gave her the O.K. sign, and she smiled a little.

Opal presented her gift first. It was an etiquette book. "I earned it washing dishes for Grandma." Opal said, and then we knew she was really joking that other time. Milt gave his mother some keen stationery. Annabelle had a white scarf. All the Moms got keen things.

At last it was my turn.

Mom spoke up. "I guess Rupert hasn't a gift for me. I—"

"Oh, yes, he has," said Miss Carlman.

I brought the bag. First, I had to explain. "I didn't buy my gift," I said. "To be honest, I found it, and it was so sad-looking that I took it home. I earned some money, but I had to spend it for some grain, so now I am very happy to present my mother with this Mother's Day rabbit."

I took it out of the bag, and plopped it in Mom's lap, and someone yelled.

"O-o-o-oh, Rupert! You darling! Oh, what a happy, happy day!"

It was not Mom. It was Mrs. Pipgrass, and she was hugging me with one arm and picking up the rabbit out of Mom's lap with the other hand.

She was explaining too. "Mr. Pipgrass bought a pair of chinchillas! I took them out for air, although he warned me not to! And this one got lost! I was afraid to advertise or tell anyone. Mr. Pipgrass is coming home tonight — and — and — I've been simply frantic! Rupert, I'm going to give you five dollars—"

"Oh, no, Mrs. Pipgrass!" Mom said. "Rupert is delighted that he can help you!"

"Well, then, here's the money for the grain — and two dollars for Rupert," Mrs. Pipgrass said. "And, Miss Carlman, do send some boys out for ice cream for everyone! My treat — in Rupert's honor. Oh, I'm so happy!" She began to cry to prove it.

So we had ice cream, and Annabelle kept wasting smiles on me.

The guys stayed to clean up.

When I got home, Mom was cooking supper. I said, "Mom, I feel terrrible because I didn't get you a gift."

Mom hugged me. "How could you? I didn't pay back your dollar."

"Mom, that's your gift — the dollar you owe me," I said. "You buy something you like — cold and quiet, or warm and wiggly."

She hugged me harder. "I have something I like that's warm and wiggly," Mom said. "And I'm hugging him right now!"

Meaning me!

These Moms!

The Very Fine Lady

THE GUYS in the sixth grade were happy, our school was getting a new stove, until Smart Annabelle and Beautiful Sylvia dreamed up their dear-little-thank-you-note idea.

All the girls were very happy, because it was worky. Work makes girls happy, and that's O.K. But they try to share their great happiness with others, and that is not O.K.

Miss Carlman made the first announcement. "Boys and girls, as you know, Mrs. Henry Van Miller won a baking contest and received one thousand dollars and a beautiful new electric stove. Mrs. Van Miller used to go to our school and she still loves it, and is a member of the P.T.A. So she is giving the stove to our school."

Everybody clapped. Then Miss Carlman went on. "At the next P.T.A. meeting, we are going to present a lovely bouquet of flowers to Mrs. Van Miller."

Annabelle raised her hand. "Miss Carlman, wouldn't it be lovely if everyone in our class would write a thank-you note to Mrs. Van Miller?"

Clayte whispered, "Vote no on this one, Piper."

"Clayte Snow and Rupert Piper — quiet," Miss Carlman said. "Yes, Milton?"

Milt stood up. "Some of the guys are very poor writers," he said. "In fact, they cannot read their own writing. It would be very unkind to make poor Mrs. Van Miller strain her eyes. One note would be enough."

Annabelle waved. She wasted a big smile on Milt. "That is a very darling idea, Milty," she said. "Miss Carlman, couldn't we have a contest? The writer of the best note will present the flowers to Mrs. Van Miller."

"An excellent idea!" said Miss Carlman. "I am proud to know that the sixth grade is really thankful. Ready for recess."

The guys went down to the "No Dames" corner, and Dood made a speech. "So now we are Emily Posts," he said. "We have to write sweet little letters, with periods and commas! Why couldn't we just say 'thank you,' and forget it?"

"I have been doing some thinking," Milt said. "We do not have to strain our brains. Who wants to present the dear little flowers to Mrs. Van Miller? Don't all speak at once!"

"That is a job for a girl," I said. "Annabelle would

like it, because she would get a new dress. And Sylvia pins her hair on forty pins, when she is going to show off."

"O.K.," Clayte said. "Then we will simply be very kind and let some girl write the best note."

Milt said, "I will read all the guys' notes. Then we will be sure that no boy's note is better than the girls'. We do not wish to break any girl's heart."

So I wrote my note at home. Mom and Gwen were talking about the stove.

Mom said, "The old stove is a disgrace. And after that creamed cabbage was burned up in the oven, no one could get the smell out."

"Isn't Mrs. Van Miller wonderful?" Gwen said.

"She certainly is," said Mom. "If Marion West had won that stove, she would have sold it and would have put the money on her back."

"What does that mean?" I said.

"Rupert Piper," Mom said, "I was not talking to you."

I went on writing. But I heard Gwen say: "You are right, Mother, Mrs. West would have bought a mink stole to drape about her lovely figure."

"And Anne Cleereman!" Mom said. "If Anne had won, we would have seen some new diamond earrings dangling from her shell-pink ears."

Gwen giggled. "She would never take a baking prize. She cooks out of a can."

"What does that mean?" I said.

"Rupert Piper," Gwen said, "you tend to your homework."

So Dad spoke up. "Well, Ila Peters and Mildred Thompson are very good with the can opener too.

Many nights they rush home and open a can of beans and a tin of cold meat, and that's what Bill and Charlie have for supper — after a hard day at the office, and a slim snack at noon."

"Piffle!" Mom said. "I have seen some of their slim snacks when I had lunch downtown. Bill's favorite snack is a turkey dinner, and Charlie's is a steak. Besides," Mom said, "we are gossiping. We are interrupting Rupert's homework."

The guys met in the "No Dames" corner, and Milt read our notes. He sat on a stone with a box for a desk.

Clayte's note said: "Dear Mrs. Van Miller: I sure thank you for the new stove. It sure is keen. Clayton."

"O.K.," Milt said. "You're safe, Clayte."

Dood's note said: "Dear Mrs. Van Miller: I did not see the new stove yet, but thanks just the same. Very truly yours, Trowbridge."

All the guys' notes were safe.

Milt read mine last. When he read it, he moaned. "You're safe, Piper! That is a very terrible note. It will make the ladies mad, and Miss Carlman will not even read it. Congratulations!"

"Thanks," I said. "Now, you'd better let us read yours."

So we read Milt's note. It said: "Dear Mrs. Van Miller: Thank you for the keen stove. It is very keen. Milton."

So Milt was safe.

We gave our notes to Miss Carlman. She read them out loud. Sylvia wrote: "Dear Mrs. Van Miller: Thank you for the charming stove. It makes our kitchen look very sweet. Sylvia."

Opal wrote: "Dear Mrs. Van Miller: Our old stove smelled so terrible ever since Miss Rockletter burned the terrible-smelling cabbage in it, and the whole kitchen has smelled so terrible—"

"A-hem!" said Miss Carlman. "I don't believe Miss Rockletter would like your note, Opal."

Then she read Annabelle's note. "Dear Mrs. Van Miller: Thank you for the lovely stove. The old stove was very hard on Miss Rockletter's nerves and she was growing old and gray—"

"A-hem!" said Miss Carlman. "Let's look at another."

She left mine for last because the writing was so bad. "You will have to read it, Rupert," she said.

So I read my note. It said: "Dear Mrs. Van Miller: Thank you for the keen stove. You are a very fine lady. Some ladies cannot cook enough to win a cooking contest. They hurry home and open a can of beans and a tin of meat and that is why their starving husbands have to get a steak downtown. Also, some ladies do not love their dear old school. They would sell the stove and buy some diamonds to dangle on their shell-pink ears, or else they would buy a mink stole to drape about their lovely figures. So thank you for the keen stove. You are a very fine lady. Yours truly, Rupert."

I finished reading and winked at the guys.

But Miss Carlman said: "A very fresh idea, Rupert! Congratulations! That is the best note, and you will present our flowers to Mrs. Van Miller."

My teeth almost dropped out. So did Milt's.

Annabelle wasted a big smile on me. So did Miss Carlman.

I did not smile back. I whispered to Milt. "You got me into this. Get me out."

So Milt stood up. "Miss Carlman," he said. "Rupert is a keen friend. But a sixth-grade boy is a very homely guy. His hair will not slick down, and he is all teeth. Also, his clothes always look very funny. I mean, his belt will not stay up."

Milt took a long breath and shut his eyes because what he was going to say next was very painful.

He said: "Miss Carlman, girls are very beautiful creatures. They frizzle their hair and they wear flowers on their pony tails and they know how to flip their eyelashes. Also, there is never any egg on their dresses. All the guys would like it if some very lovely girl would present the flowers to Mrs. Van Miller."

Miss Carlman laughed out loud. "A nice try, Milton," she said. "But all my boys are nice-looking boys, and Rupert will make a speech and present the flowers."

So I had to practice in our garage. And the guys came to hear me. "You are not too good," Milt said. "Rupert, you do not have anyone to take the place of Mrs. Van Miller. That is your trouble."

So I got an idea. I went over to see Mrs. Van Miller. "May I please borrow one of your hats?" I said.

"My hat?" She looked very surprised.

"I need it — to practice," I said.

So she gave me her hat with a feather on it, but she looked puzzled.

Our old clothesline pole was in the garage. So I painted a little face on it, and I put the hat on its head, and that was Mrs. Van Miller.

Every day after school I picked dandelions and went

to the garage and presented them to this wooden lady.

On Thursday, I heard someone laugh — and there was Mrs. Van Miller.

"Rupert," she said, "who is your charming friend?"

"Well," I said, "you see, I am scared."

"I used to be scared," she said. "When I was your age, I could not sleep at night if I had to make a speech before grownups. I'm a little bit scared to stand up and receive those flowers."

Then she looked at the wooden lady and laughed again.

"Let's practice!" she said. She took the hat off the clothesline pole and put it on her own head. "There! Now you will feel at home."

So I made my speech and gave her the dandelions, and she thanked me. We practiced six times.

P.T.A. was the next day. Mrs. Van Miller was very dressed up, and I was almost scared to look at her.

But I did look, and she was laughing, and I almost laughed too.

Because Mrs. Van Miller was wearing the hat that I had put on the clothesline pole. She wore it so that I would not be scared. She did it because she is a very fine lady.

So I made my speech and gave her the flowers, and someone took our pictures. Then we had ice cream and cake. The cake was made from Mrs. Van Miller's prize recipe.

"Isn't it delicious, Rupert?" Annabelle said.

"Yes," I said. "Only a very fine lady can make a cake like this."

So Annabelle flipped her eyelashes at me and went over and asked Mrs. Van Miller for the recipe.

A Dish for a Man

DURING the last week of school, Miss Carlman had very keen news for us. Bill (Cowpoke) Harrison, the cowboy singer, was coming to our town to sing.

"In the afternoon he will be the special guest of the sixth grade and the sixth-grade mothers," Miss Carlman said. "I am sure we all feel very honored. Please tell your mothers tonight."

So I told mine. "Mom, the sixth-grade mothers got rooked to fix the eats, Thursday afternoon."

"Why the sixth grade, Rupert?" my sister Gwen, asked.

"Because Cowpoke never got farther than fifth," my dad said. "He will think he is promoted. Ha! Ha!"

Mom said: "That is not true at all! Rupert Piper, don't you tell anyone what Daddy said. Bill Harrison is a college graduate, and under his cowboy shirt and boots he is a person of culture and refinement."

My backbone turned cold. "You mean he's a sissy!" I said.

Mom put her cup down hard. "Honestly, you Piper men!" she said.

The next morning Miss Carlman said: "We have Mrs. Van Miller's lovely new stove, and we have not done much cooking in it. The mothers think it would be nice for the sixth grade to prepare refreshments when William Harrison comes."

She meant Cowpoke.

Clayte nudged me. "Watch this, Piper," he whispered. "It could get worky."

Smart Annabelle raised her hand. "I think the lunch should look very pretty," she said.

Beautiful Sylvia waved. "I think we should have dainty sandwiches," she said. "And little bits of cakes with colored icing. And lace napkins."

I waved. "Miss Carlman," I said, "a cowboy likes meat and potatoes and gravy. And paper napkins."

Milt said, "The guys — I mean the boys — all vote for meat and potatoes and gravy."

Smart Annabelle tried to turn pale. "This is a party," she said. "We should have party food. Also, Mr. Harrison is not a real cowboy. He is a singer."

Opal waved. "Miss Carlman," she said, "Mr. Cowpoke Harrison is an artist. Artists do not eat the way men do. Artists eat very delicate food, and most of them have ulcers."

Well, we voted, and there were fifteen girls and fourteen boys, so the dear little sandwiches won.

At recess we went down to the "No Dames" corner to do our worrying.

"You might know!" Milt said. "Poor old Cowpoke!"

"If Cowpoke is a real he-man," Clayte said, "he will prefer to bite his own sandwiches. He will not wish them all cut up bite-size for him."

Dood was very sad. "We will never know whether Cowpoke is a real he-man or not," he said. "He will not have a chance, the poor guy. There will be nothing to eat but little pieces of bread with a dib of cheese and a dab of jelly. I could eat a whole plateful and still be hungry."

Just then a car stopped beside the schoolyard. It was Bob Quillon, the photographer for the *Gazette,* and a very good guy.

"Hey!" he yelled. "Why all the fun and laughter?"

We ran over to talk to him. We told him about the lunch for Cowpoke.

"H'm!" he said. "I know just what you mean, men. I am often invited to take pictures for some dear ladies, and they wish me to eat a few of their darling little sandwiches and cakes. It's all right if a man is not hungry. A man could eat two dozen of those sandwiches and then sit right down and starve to death."

"That's what Cowpoke will do," said Milt.

"That isn't the worst," Dood said. "He will starve to death with a lace napkin on his knee."

"A terrible fate for a cowpoke," Bob said. "Men, this calls for action. You men meet me in Aunt Trudy's basement at seven o'clock, after Aunt Trudy has

gone to her meeting. We will make a dish that is fit
for a man and see what Cowpoke does about it. We
will give him a chance to show whether he is a he-
man or just a singer."

Bob lives with his aunt, Mrs. Wheelock. So he took
her to her meeting, and then we all went down into
her basement. There is a stove down there.

"It's for cooking in summer or for cooking smelly
things," Bob said. "We are going to make something
that is a dish for a man. We are going to make chili."

Bob had two kettles that were as big as tubs.
We opened cans and cans of tomatoes and tomato
juice and big red beans and we emptied them into the
kettles and put chili powder in them.

"Men don't use recipes," Bob said. "They taste until it's right."

We peeled onions and cut them up small. Bob
brought two big frying pans. We put raw ground
meat in them and salted it and mixed in the onions.
We cooked the meat until it was brown and then we
put it in the kettles.

"Now," Bob said, "we'll just drop a clove of garlic
in each kettle."

When the kettles were bubbling, we boiled water and
put salt in it and cooked a lot of spaghetti. After it was
cooked, we washed the starch out of it. We put it in the
kettles and cooked it all just a little while longer.

"Now!" Bob said. "Let's taste it to be sure it's a dish
for a man."

It was a dish for a man. It tasted like more, but we
did not eat much.

"We'll need it tomorrow," Bob said.

The next afternoon Cowpoke came to school. He was tall and he looked just like his pictures. He sang for the school and the mothers, and then it was time for lunch.

"Children, bring the trays from the kitchen," Miss Carlman said.

The trays were covered with sandwiches and cakes.

"Aren't they darling? Aren't they cutie-bug?" Annabelle said.

"Some lunch for Cowpoke!" Milt said. "No meat and potatoes and gravy."

"I hope not!" said Sylvia. "He would think we are not cultured and refined."

Well, Cowpoke put his lace napkin on his knee. Annabelle passed him the tray of sandwiches. The guys waited to see him get mad.

But Cowpoke smiled and took two sandwiches. "These look delightful!" he said.

My teeth almost dropped out.

"Rupert," Miss Carlman said, "bring up a few more cups."

On the stairs I met Bob Quillon. "We wasted our time," I said. "Cowpoke is a sissy after all. He is eating the sandwiches and he does not even look mad. He is not a he-man."

"I've eaten lots of those sandwiches and I am a he-man," Bob whispered. "Cowpoke has to be a gentleman. We'll give him a chance."

I took the cups into our room. In a minute, the door opened again and Bob Quillon was there with his camera. He held the door open, and a delicious smell came into the room.

It was our chili. We could smell the elegant onions and garlic. I could shut my eyes and see the beautiful fat beans swimming around in the tomatoes and spaghetti and meat.

"Bob," said Mrs. Hall, "what in the world is that smell?"

Mrs. Willman said, "Have you just come from a restaurant?"

"No," Bob said, "I brought my lunch along." He looked at the little sandwiches. "I'm on a diet," he said. He winked at Cowpoke.

Cowpoke put down his plate and walked over to the door and sniffed.

"It's just this silly old stuff," Bob said. "Doctor's orders." He lifted the kettle cover.

Cowpoke smiled. "You know," he said, "I hated to mention it but I'm on a diet too. The same diet. Doctor's orders. Sad case!"

The guys were sad cases too. We were so hungry we were almost dead. We wanted to say it was doctor's orders too, but our moms would hear.

"Miss Carlman," Bob Quillon said, "may we poor sufferers have some soup bowls? We'll eat down in the kitchen, of course, so we can discuss our sad cases."

It was very, very silent in the room.

Then Miss Smithwick stood up. I shook a little, and Smart Annabelle flipped her eyelashes at me.

Miss Smithwick walked tappety-tappety-tap over to the door and sniffed. I shook some more.

But Miss Smithwick said: "Come to think of it, I'm on a diet too. Let's bring the soup bowls up here."

So we brought the bowls, and everyone was on a diet, even the mothers and Miss Carlman.

"That's your third bowl of chili, Annabelle," I said. "Cowpoke will think you're not cultured and refined."

"How about your cutie-bug sandwiches?" Milt said.

Sylvia said: "Oh, we can eat them later. Rupert, who made this chili?"

"We guys made it," I said.

"It is delicious," said Annabelle. She smiled at me. "I wish my dad could make chili just like it."

"Married men with wives do not have time for things like this, and that is why I am always going to be a single man."

"Me too," said Milt and Clayte and Dood, all in one breath.

The girls just wasted some more smiles on us, and then Cowpoke Harrison took his guitar and sang us another song, and we all sang the chorus with him.

Long Live the Queen

SUMMER vacation had finally arrived, but you'd never know it. No work at school means more work at home, I guess.

Anyway, it was a very hot day and everything was melting except some people's very hard hearts.

We were sitting on my front step, talking about our troubles and our empty pockets. "A fine thing!" Milt said. "The fair is coming, and we do not have any money."

"We are supposed to earn it," said Dood. "But it is too hot to labor."

"My right foot hurts," said Clayte. "But does that melt my mom's heart? Oh, no! Not hers! I am supposed to limp and hop to the store and get some bread. Look." Clayte went hippety-hop over to the sidewalk.

He held up his foot and rubbed it. "Ow-oo!" he said. "Ow-oo! I might die!"

"That is your left foot," I said. "You said it was your right foot that hurts. Make up your mind."

"Don't get funny, Rupert Piper," Clayte said. "I did not say that my left foot does not hurt, too."

"Well, does it?" Dood said.

"It sure does! Oh, how I suffer!" Clayte lay down on his back and held both feet up in the air, and moaned.

"Your mother is out on your porch looking for you, Clayte," Milt said.

"She is not looking for her poor, suffering boy," Clayte said. "She is looking for her bread."

"My mom is the same," I said. "She knows when our basement needs sweeping, but does she know when her son's pitching arm has a very bad sore on it? Oh, no!" I held up my arm, and groaned.

Milt winked at me, so I knew he could see Ma in the doorway. He said, "That's bad, Piper. That arm might drop off, any time." He poked it a little. "A little exercise, like sweeping, might be fatal," he said.

"You're wasting time," Dood said. "She's gone."

"It would not melt her heart, anyway," Clayte said. His mother was calling him. "There is no way out," he said. "I will have to hobble to the store, with my dying breath."

"Crawl on your hands," Dood said. "That might make her sorry."

"Wait a minute!" Milt said. "Men, we will carry our dear, dying friend Clayte to the store, and back."

"A very good idea," I said.

So Milt and I made a seat with our hands, and Clayte sat down on it and put his arms around our necks.

Dood walked behind. "I am the spare tire," he said. When we passed Clayte's house, his mother was on the porch, shaking rugs. Clayte moaned a little.

His mother smiled. "My, aren't we having fun, this nice morning! Don't forget the bread, Clayton."

"I am going after it, Ma," Clayte said. "Slow, but sure. Dead, or alive."

"That's sweet," she said. She hummed a little, and went in.

"Look, Clayte, you weigh a ton." I said. "It's time to use the spare tire."

"Put me down easy," Clayte said. He moaned a terrible moan.

So Doodleberries took my place and I walked behind, to the store. We got the bread. Then Dood and I carried Clayte, and Milt carried the bread.

Clayte's mother was shaking another rug. "Still having fun!" she said. "And you've brought the bread!"

"It is a deed of mercy, Mrs. Snow," Milt said. He wiped his face on his sleeve. "We could not let Clayte hobble and hop so far on his lame feet."

"Lame feet?" Mrs. Snow said. "Clayton Snow, what's wrong with your feet?"

"Oh, nothing," Clayte said. "There's nothing wrong with my feet, Mom. They hurt, because I have got stones in my shoes."

"Stones!" His mom stared at him. We stared some, too. His mom said. "You have stones in your shoes — and you let these poor boys carry you to the store — Oh, dear, there's the telephone!" Mrs. Snow went in the house.

We stared at Clayte some more. He put his hands in his pockets and whistled.

"Some lazy guy!" I said.

"Too lazy to shake the stones out of your shoes," Dood said.

"Well," Clayte said, "you didn't ask me. And you gave me a bumpy ride, too."

"Say that again!" I said. "You just say that again! After I carried you on this sore arm. Look at this arm! Wait. I don't see the mosquito bite. I guess it's the other arm."

Right then Beautiful Sylvia and Opal and Smart Annabelle came along, with popsickles. They were swishing along, pretending it was a lovely, cool day.

When the girls saw me with my sleeve rolled up and my fist in Clayte's face, they tried to faint on the sidewalk.

"Rupert!" Opal said, through her nose. "Oh, Rupert, please don't strike Claytie! Let's settle this peacefully!"

"Don't spoil our day with blood," Sylvia said. "We are so happy because we are going to win a beauty contest, maybe."

We were a little bit mad, and this made us madder.

"Hah!" Dood said. "Beauty contest! Hah! How can you win a beauty contest with those eyelashes, Annabelle?"

Milt looked at Sylvia, "And how can you win, with that hair?"

I said, "Opal will get one vote."

The guys knew who I meant. Opal's dad thinks Opal is very beautiful.

"Hah!" I said. "Clayte is prettier than you girls!" I said this because I was mad at Clayte. Not very mad, but a little.

Annabelle flipped her eyelashes at me. "You'll be sorry!" she said. "You'll all be sorry, when we are Junior Cheese Queen, and her Court, with free passes to the fair to give away, and little gifts to give away, too. You will be sorry that you are just some old boys who think we look ugly, and not our dear friends."

The girls went away, and Clayte said. "So I'm pretty! What do you mean?"

"Why, it is your lovely eyelashes," Dood said. "And your rosy lips."

"It is your dreamy eyes," Milt said.

We thought Clayte would get mad, but he was feeling smart about his free ride.

"Well," he said, "I am not so beautiful, but I think I am prettier than Annabelle." Then he ran into his house.

Our mothers caught us and we had to work, and we forgot about the beauty contest.

Friday night the Junior Cheese Queen's pictures was in the newspaper. It said: MYSTERY GIRL IS CHOSEN QUEEN.

Then it said: "An unknown Sixth Grader has won the title of JUNIOR CHEESE QUEEN. Above is her picture at the age of one, chosen by the judges as the prettiest of those entered. However, the Queen forgot to send her name. Will she please appear at the Fair Office, to claim her picture and receive instructions?"

"That's very strange," my dad said. "How did they work this thing?"

My sister Gwen spoke up. "Well, all the dairy companies are sponsoring it. It is for Sixth Graders. They sent in their baby pictures, with their names in sealed envelopes so that the judging would be fair. The one who was the prettiest baby will be Queen, and she can choose her Court. They will have free passes to the fair every day, and good seats for everything, besides lots of gifts."

Mom looked at the picture. "Is that Annabelle?" I said.

"No," Mom said. "It looks very familiar, but it is not Annabelle or Sylvia or Opal. I remember them all, as babies. In fact, I have all their baby pictures."

"Hah!" I said. "We told them they could not win. We told them old Clayte was prettier!"

"Clayton?" Mom said. She began to laugh. "Well, you were right. This is Clayton!"

Poor old Clayte! He was elected Cheese Queen! "I guess he sent his baby picture for fun," I said. "He did not think he would be Queen."

The next morning Milt said, "This is a very great disgrace. I'll bet Clayte is hiding in his attic."

"Well," I said, "long live the Queen! We are still his friends. We will still speak to him, if no one is looking."

"Let's go tell him," Dood said.

We hurried over to Clayte's house and rang the bell. Mrs. Snow came to the door.

"Mrs. Snow," Milt said sadly, "we have arrived to offer our sympathy. Where is the Beauty Queen hiding out?"

I punched Milt.

"Excuse me!" he said. "I mean, where is Clayte?"

"Clayton? Oh, he went down town," Mrs. Snow said.

So we went down town and when we passed the Fair Office there was Clayte inside, standing in front of the desk, talking to Mr. Schilling.

"Mr. Schilling looks worried," Dood said. "I guess Clayte is telling him this is all a mistake."

We went in. "Long live the Queen!" Dood yelled.

"Hi!" Clayte said. He did not look disgraced. He said, "Mr. Schilling, here are Rupert and Milt and Dood. When I am Queen, I would like to choose them to be my Court."

Our teeth almost dropped out.

Mr. Schilling looked at a little paper. He bit his thumbnail. "Well," he said, "there is nothing in these rules that says they can't be the Court. Let's see, "Open to Sixth Graders." Someone slipped. It should have been Sixth-Grade girls. Clayte, are you sure you want to be Queen?"

"I am no quitter," Clayte said. "We will take our free passes, now, please."

"Someone slipped," Mr. Schilling said again. "Well, here are your passes, boys."

We started home, and we met Annabelle and Sylvia and Opal. "Well," Clayte said, "the guys told you I am prettier than you. And I am. You are looking at the Cheese Queen and the Court."

"Yah!" I said. "Long live the Queen!"

"How silly," Annabelle said. "Clayton Snow, a boy can't be Queen."

"The rules said the beauty contest was open to Sixth Graders," Clayte said. "I am a Sixth Grader and I am Queen. As I glide past you on my lovely float, I will toss you a rose."

Opal giggled. "Claytie, you will look very sweet in your white dress."

Sylvia said, "Milt and Rupert and Dood will be adorable in blue and pink and yellow dresses with flowers in their hair."

"We don't have to wear dresses," Clayte said. "I will wear my own clothes. So will my Court."

So Opal stopped giggling. "Claytie," she said, "I was second, in the contest."

"Honestly, she was!" Annabelle said. "Opal was a beautiful baby. Clayte, if you were a hero, you would resign. Then Opal would be Queen, and we would be her Court."

"I am no quitter," Clayte said. "And what would my dear, dear friends get out of it?"

"Well," Opal said, "you are our friends, too. The Queen and her Court can give a few free passes and some gifts to a few friends. We would give ours to you."

"The Queen resigns!" Clayte said. "It's a deal!" He made a big bow to Opal. He said, "Long Live the Queen!"

This was just what Clayte wanted. He is not dumb, even if he is a little lazy, sometimes.

We went to the fair for free. Queen Opal and her Court gave us some little cheeses and some ice-cream bars and chocolate milk, and some very sweet smiles when they rode past on their float.

"Clayte," I said, "you were a very smart guy, to send your baby picture to the contest."

"Well," Clayte said, "I am not too smart, but I am honest. I will tell you the truth. My mom sent the picture, just for fun, because she thinks I was the prettiest baby that ever was born. Mothers only pretend to have hard hearts. They are very queer, mushy people."

"Very true," we said. "Very true."

One for the Univac

I DON'T know whose idea it was to make friends with Albert Einstein Smedley. That's one to ask the Univac.

"Rupert," my mother said at breakfast, "what in the world are you dreaming about?"

"Oh, not much," I said. "I was thinking about something that is reposing in Miss Smithwick's alley."

"Oh, dear!" Mom said. "I might have known!"

"What's in the alley, Rupert?" Dad said.

"Well," I said, "Miss Smithwick's old piano box is in the alley."

Mom looked at Dad and shook her head. "Why do you suppose it is?" she said. "We are as smart as Don and Irene Smedley. Why would their child be a second Einstein, while ours dreams great dreams about a piano box in an alley?"

"That," Dad said, "is one for the Univac."

This was a very good answer. A Univac is an electric machine that can answer anything. You just feed the question into it and it buzzes and whirs and little lights blink, and after a while out pops the answer.

I ate my Pop-O's and drank my milk. "Excuse me," I said.

Mom said, "Where are you going?"

"Well, to find the guys."

"Naturally! And then where?"

"Mom," I said, "that's a toughie. That is one for the Univac."

Mom looked at Dad. "Now!" she said. "See what you started, Mr. Piper! Rupert, if you have any notion of bringing that piano box home, you get it right out of your head — while the Smedleys are visiting in town! I won't have Mrs. Smedley saying that our son is a trash-picker!"

I hated to tell the fellows. So I waited until afternoon, when we were sitting out back of our garage, on the piano box.

"How did your mom know what we were going to do?" Milt said.

I said, "That's one for the Univac."

"Well," Clayte said, "we will not take up any of her yard. All her troubles will be over, as soon as we get this good old piano box up in this tree."

"Right!" Dood said. "But how are we going to do it?"

Just then a car came down our drive. It was Opal's father, Mr. Duncan. "Hello, gentlemen!" he said. "Rupert, your dad said he'd leave some fishing tackle in the garage where a real fisherman could borrow it. Hey! What's this?" He looked at the piano box. Next, he looked up in the tree, and smiled a very big smile. "A very good idea!" he said. "If you'll wait until to-morrow I'll help you put it up there."

He got the fishing tackle and drove away.

"How did he know?" Milt said.

"Well," I said, "he is an electrical engineer. Maybe he has a Univac."

Right then, Mom called me. "Rupert? Rupert Piper! Come here!"

"Oh — oh!" Clayte said. "I knew this would happen!"

But Mom was not mad. We had company. It was Smart Annabelle and her mother, and Mrs. Smedley and Albert.

"Here's the croquet set, Rupert," Mom said. "Have a nice game."

"Well," Dood said, "I think I will be going."

"Me, too," said Milt and Clayte.

Mom smiled very sweetly. "Your mothers are drop-ping in, boys. They expect to find you here — playing croquet." She shut the door.

Albert was taking a little stroll in the yard, looking at things and smelling our flowers.

Annabelle said, "Albert simply has to get away by himself, to dream great dreams. His mother says so. She wishes he would share his great thoughts with mankind. But she says some day the world will know, when Albert has his private chain of satellites around the sun."

Well, we did not want a satellite around the sun. All we wanted was a house in the tree.

Albert came back, looking excited. "Rupert," he said, "What is that big box doing, back of your garage?"

"Well," I said, "I guess that is one for the Univac."

"Univac?" Albert said. "You can't make a Univac out of a piano box!"

Milt poked me. "Oh, indeed you can!" Milt said. "You can, Albert, if you know enough science. And we do!" Milt put his hands in his pockets and kind of rocked on his heels and smacked. He said, "Our Univac will be just about the best Univac in the U.S.A. It will answer all questions correctly within five minutes — or your money back."

My teeth almost dropped out. So did Dood's and Clayte's.

Albert's face was very red. He said, "I have a fine laboratory at home. It cost hundreds of dollars! But I cannot make a Univac."

"You do not need a laboratory, to build a Univac," Milt said. "You just need to know how," he smacked. "And we do."

So the next morning we were working very hard in my backyard when Annabelle came along with Beautiful Sylvia and Opal and Albert.

The girls stopped to ask a few very personal questions. "What in the world are you boys doing with that old sweeper and old beat-up fan and old dog clipper?" Opal said, through her nose.

"Or is it a secret?" Sylvia said.

"Oh, no," I said. "We are willing to share our great thoughts with mankind. However, most of you happen to be girls."

Annabelle flipped her eyelashes at me. "Come on, Albert," she said.

But Albert stood still. "Excuse me," he said. "I think I shall stay and learn how to build a Univac."

So every day we worked on the Univac. Mr. Duncan helped us sometimes.

"I do not want all the boys in town to get fatal electric shocks and die," he said. "I have a daughter to marry off some day."

He meant Opal. I peeked at Milt under my eyelids. Clayte and Dood and Albert were peeking at us, too. Dood began to whistle.

Mr. Duncan is very crazy about Opal, and we did not want to hurt his feelings and tell him we do not plan to marry her.

He fixed all the Christmas tree lights in the Univac. He worked on the old sweeper and the fan and the old dog clipper. He tested all the cords and connections so that no one would get a shock.

We painted the Univac a very keen green color.

On Thursday we moved it onto our lawn.

After a while Mom walked home from her club meeting with Albert's mother and all the other mothers, and you should have heard Mom scream.

"What is that horrible thing on my lawn? It looks like a prospector's hut, or an ice fisher's shanty!"

"No, ma'am," I said. "Please read the sign, ma'am."

The sign read:

UNIVAC, INC.
ANSWERS ANY QUESTIONS — 5 CENTS
NOT RESPONSIBLE

"I give up!" Mom said. "What did I ever do to deserve this?"

"Do you wish to ask the Univac?" I said. "Write it on this piece of paper, and slip it in here, with a nickel."

So Mom put the question in the Univac. All the little lights began to wink and blink. The sweeper motor ran. The fan whirled. The dog clipper whirred. Everything made a terrible noise.

After a while the noise slowed up and another slot opened and out came the answer.

The answer was: DON'T WORRY, MRS. PIPER. THIS WILL MAKE A LOT OF MONEY.

Mom laughed. "Well, well! That's different! Do any of you ladies care to try the Univac?"

"It's amusing," Mrs. Smedley said. "However, Albert would be bored with any toy as childish as this."

Mom's cheeks got kind of pink. So did the other mothers'.

"I'll ask it something," Clayte's mother said. So she found a nickel and then she wrote, "What can I fix quick for supper?"

The lights blinked and the machines all roared, and the answer came out: BAKE SOME FROZEN CHICKEN PIES. CLAYTE CAN EAT TWO.

"An excellent idea!" Mrs. Snow said. "Marvelous!"

Dood's mother said, "I'll ask it something, to see if it's honest." So she wrote a note: "Who is the smartest boy I know?"

The Univac almost shook to pieces and then the answer came: HE IS THE BOY WHO LIKES YOU BEST.

"How sweet!" Mrs. Hall said. "Thank you, Univac!"

Mrs. Willman dug a nickel out of her purse. She wrote: "Is Annabelle going to do the dishes tonight?"

This was a toughie. But the answer was good. Very good. THE PRETTIEST AND SMARTEST GIRL AT YOUR HOUSE IS GOING TO DO THE DISHES, TELL ANNABELLE.

"I'll try it, Univac," Mrs. Willman said. "If it doesn't work, I might try something else." She slapped her hands together, and then laughed.

The Dad's Club Carnival was the next night. Mr. Duncan came around at four o'clock.

"Rupert," he said, "how about moving the Univac down to the carnival? We can pick up some extra cash."

"Oh, keen!" I said. "The cash is for the camp fund."

"Bring your crew of great scientists," Mr. Duncan said, "they will get some free ice cream and pop tickets."

Well, the Univac was so busy that our crew of great scientists had to take turns working and eating.

After a while Mrs. Smedley came along. "Where on earth is Albert?" she said. "I haven't seen that boy since I got here!"

Right then Mr. Duncan came up. "Hello there, Mrs. Smedley," he said. "What do you think of the Univac?"

"It's very silly," she said.

Mr. Duncan smiled. "Come, now. It's a lot of fun. You ask Albert."

Mrs. Smedley kind of sniffed. "Albert wouldn't be interested. He's going to be a brilliant scientist."

"Well!" Mr. Duncan said. "What has he made?"

"Why, nothing — yet. He's learning."

"Then," Mr. Duncan said, "you'll be proud to know he helped make this Univac."

Mrs. Smedley tried to turn white. "I don't believe it!" she said.

Mr. Duncan winked at me. "Rupert," he said, "I'll risk a nickel on Albert. Ask the Univac where he is."

So I wrote: "Where is Albert?"

The poor old Univac almost blew a fuse, and after a while the answer came: I AM VERY BUSY. DON'T WORRY ABOUT ME!

Mrs. Smedley screamed. "Is Albert in that contraption?"

"He sure is!" Mr. Duncan said. "My old typewriter is in there, and Albert is writing up these answers, and having himself a ball. Of course, it's a scientific secret."

"That's right, Mrs. Smedley," I said. "Next, it's Albert's turn to run the sweeper and the fan."

"And if you want to break his heart — you stop him!" Mr. Duncan said.

Mrs. Smedley stood and watched the Univac a long time. It was very busy.

At last Mrs. Smedley said, "Give me a piece of paper, Rupert."

She wrote a question. "Would the Univac like a hamburger?"

The Univac shook. The lights blinked. The answer came: THE UNIVAC WOULD LIKE FIVE HAM-BURGERS.

The hamburgers were very good, and Mrs. Smedley didn't even have to ask good old Univac how many bottles of pop to order.